5/14 K1

D1480661

The Lute Player

A TALE FROM RUSSIA

Retold by Suzanne I. Barchers
Illustrated by Viktor Sluzhaev

RED
CHAIR
•PRESS•

Please visit our website at **www.redchairpress.com**.
Find a free catalog of all our high-quality products for young readers.

 For a free activity page for this story, go to
www.redchairpress.com and look for Free Activities.

The Lute Player

Publisher's Cataloging-In-Publication Data
(Prepared by The Donohue Group, Inc.)

Barchers, Suzanne I.
The lute player : a tale from Russia / retold by Suzanne I. Barchers ; illustrated by Viktor
Sluzhaev.
p. : col. ill. ; cm. -- (Tales of honor)
Summary: The king, who loves adventures, is imprisoned during one of his long journeys.
When the queen sets out to find her husband, she must travel in disguise. This is a tale of
love, devotion, and ingenuity from the days of medieval Russia. Includes special educational
sections: Words to know, What do you think?, and About Russia.
Interest age level: 006-010.
ISBN: 978-1-937529-75-8 (lib. binding/hardcover)
ISBN: 978-1-937529-59-8 (pbk.)
ISBN: 978-1-936163-91-5 (eBook)
1. Devotion--Juvenile fiction. 2. Queens--Juvenile fiction. 3. Disguise--Juvenile fiction.
4. Lutenists--Juvenile fiction. 5. Folklore--Russia. 6. Love--Fiction. 7. Kings, queens, rulers,
etc.--Fiction. 8. Disguise--Fiction. 9. Musicians--Fiction. 10. Folklore--Russia. I. Sluzhaev,
Viktor. II. Title.

PZ8.1.B37 Lu 2013

398.2/73/0947   2012951561

This series first published by:
Red Chair Press LLC   PO Box 333   South Egremont, MA 01258-0333

Printed in the United States of America

1 2 3 4 5 18 17 16 15 14

Once upon a time there were a king and a queen who lived happily together. As the years passed, the king grew restless. He longed to see the world, to try his strength in battle, and to find honor and glory.

He called his army together. He gave his wife a loving embrace. Then he left with the army to a distant land of an evil king.

Upon arrival, the king and his army traveled through the country, defeating all they met for many months. Then they came to a mountain pass, where a rival army waited for him.

Overpowered, the soldiers fled and the king was taken prisoner. By night he was chained. By day he was made to plow the fields.

After three years, the king found a way to send a message to his dear queen. The letter directed her to sell all the castles, pawn the treasures, and use the money to buy his freedom.

The queen wept bitterly as she read it. "What shall I do?" she wondered. "If I go myself, I fear the evil king will keep me. I could send a maid, but how can I trust anyone with so much money?"

She thought for hours. Then she had an idea. She cut off all her beautiful long hair. She dressed herself in boy's clothes. Then she took her lute, and without saying a word to anyone, she went in search of her husband.

She traveled through many lands and saw many cities. Finally, she arrived at the place where the evil king lived. She walked all around the palace, finding the prison tower.

She returned to the front of the palace. Standing
in the great court, she took her lute in hand. She
began to play, and everyone stopped to listen.

Soon the evil king heard her sweet voice.

*I come from my own country far into this
foreign land.*

*Of all I own I take alone, my sweet lute in my
hand.*

*I sing of blooming flowers, made sweet by sun
and rain;*

*Of all the bliss of love's first kiss, and parting's
cruel pain.*

*Of the sad captive's longing, within his
prison wall,*

*Of hearts that sigh when none are nigh to
answer to their call.*

*If you hear my singing, within your palace,
sire,*

*Oh give, I pray, this happy day, to me my
heart's desire.*

The evil king heard this touching song and had the singer brought before him.

"Welcome, lute player," he said. "Where do you come from?"

"My country, sire is far away across many seas," she answered. "For years I have been wandering the world. I earn my living with my music."

"Then stay here a few days," the king said. "When you wish to leave, I will give you what you ask for in your song…your heart's desire."

So the lute player stayed on in the palace. She sang and played to the king almost all day long. He never tired of listening to the "young lad." In fact, he almost forgot to eat or drink or torment his people.

One day, he declared, "Your playing and singing make me feel as if some gentle hand lifted every care and sorrow from me."

After three days, the lute player came to take leave of the evil king. As promised he asked her what she would like as her reward.

"Sire," she said. "Give me one of your prisoners. You have so many, and I would be glad of a companion on my journeys. When I hear his voice, I shall think of you and thank you."

"Come along, then," said the king. "Choose
whom you will." And he took the player to the
prison himself.

The queen walked among the prisoners. Dressed as she was as a young boy, her husband did not recognize her, even after they were on their way. He assumed he was now the lute player's prisoner.

When they got near their country, he spoke to her. "I am no common prisoner. Let me go free and I will reward you."

"I need no reward," she answered. "Go in peace."

"Then come with me, young man. Be my guest in my home," said the grateful king.

"One day I will come to see you," she said. And so they parted.

The queen took a shorter way home, changing into her robes just before the king arrived. An hour later, people were shouting that the king had returned.

She went to meet him. He greeted everyone warmly, except for the queen. He would not even look at her.

He met with his council and said, "See what sort of wife I have? I was trapped in prison and got a message to her. Did she do anything to help me? No!"

A minister answered, saying, "Sire, when news came about your imprisonment, the queen disappeared. She just returned today."

Meanwhile the queen disguised herself with a long cloak. Slipping into the court, she began to sing. She ended as before with this refrain.

If you hear my singing, within your palace, sire,

Oh give, I pray, this happy day, to me my heart's desire.

As soon as the king heard this song he ran out and brought the lute player into the palace.

He announced to his council, "Here is the man who released me from prison!" Turning to the lute player, he said, "You are my true friend. Let me give you your heart's desire."

The queen declared, "I am sure you will not be less generous than the evil king. He offered my heart's desire and I got what I wanted—you! And I don't intend to give you up!"

She threw off her cloak. And with that, the king knew that she had indeed been the true wife he had always loved.

bliss: perfect happiness

captive: a person who has been taken prisoner

desire: something strongly wanted

lute: a stringed instrument with a long neck and round body

torment: cause extreme suffering

wandering: going aimlessly from place to place

Question 1: When the queen learned her husband was in prison, why did she not buy his freedom from the evil king? Why did she disguise herself as a boy?

Question 2: What did the evil king promise the lute player if he would stay in the palace?

Question 3: After the good king returned home, the queen played and sang for him. Why did the king not recognize his wife?

Question 4: Do you think the queen was wrong to trick the evil king into releasing his prisoner? Why or why not?

About Russia

In Russia's early history, a powerful group of kingdoms banded together as Kievan Rus. The kings and princes ruled Kievan Rus together throughout the 11th Century. In the 15th Century the grand princes expanded their lands and eventually recognized Ivan IV as the sole ruler or Tsar. *The Lute Player* is a folktale of good and evil rulers from this proud and beautiful country known today as the Russian Federation.

About the Author

After fifteen years as a teacher, Suzanne Barchers began a career in writing and publishing. She has written over 100 children's books, two college textbooks, and more than 20 reader's theater and teacher resource books. She previously held editorial roles at Weekly Reader and LeapFrog and is on the PBS Kids Media Advisory Board. Suzanne also plays the flute professionally – and for fun – from her home in Stanford, CA.

About the Illustrator

Viktor Sluzhaev, named one of the 200 best young illustrators of Russia, was born in Lgov in the Kursk region. He studied art in Dimitrovgrad and spent several years running a business selling children's illustrated literature. His time selling books led Viktor back to his passion: illustrating fairy tales and fables for young readers.